The Best Tailor in Pinbauê

For Lucas, Antonio, and Clemens,
For my brother Vincente and my father João

Original edition published under the title *Onkel Flores*.

Copyright © 2009 by Baobab Books, Basel, Switzerland
English translation © 2016 by Baobab Books

First Seven Stories Press edition October 2017.

Seven Stories Press
140 Watts Street
New York, NY 10013
www.sevenstories.com

College professors may order examination copies of Seven Stories
Press titles for free. To order, visit http://www.sevenstories.com/
textbook or send a fax on school letterhead to (212) 226-1411.

Library of Congress Cataloging-in-Publication Data on file.

ISBN: 978-1-60980-804-4 (hardcover)
ISBN: 978-1-60980-805-1 (ebook)

Printed in China

9 8 7 6 5 4 3 2 1

The Best Tailor in Pinbauê

EYMARD TOLEDO

Seven Stories Press | Triangle Square
New York • Oakland

Uncle Flores is a tailor—the best in Pinbauê. When I was a child,
I spent a lot of time with him and he taught me many things:
how to cut cloth, how to sew on buttons, how to tack. The only thing
I wasn't allowed to use was his sewing machine. It was his most
precious treasure. But I liked watching him step on the pedal and I
loved the rattling sound of the black machine when the pedal went
up and down: *Cloc cloc cloc cloc cloc.*
When I helped him to cut the
cloth, Uncle Flores told me:
"Hold it tight, Edinho,
or else it will be crooked."
Zzzzzzzzzzzzzzz. We cut
through the cloth with two
big pairs of scissors until
they met in the middle.

I would get up early in the morning and go over to Uncle Flores's
house for breakfast. When I came to his house, it was still dark.
I could hear my uncle singing from afar. He liked to sing while
he shaved. When he was done, we had coffee and bread together.
"This will help you concentrate at school," Uncle Flores would say.

After school I went back to Uncle Flores's and spent the afternoon with him. My mum only came back from work in the evening. When I was done with my homework, we sat in the kitchen and my uncle told me stories. I liked the ones best that began with *Once upon a time. . .*

"Once upon a time the nets of the pescadores* were full with fish. And the lavadeiras** laughed and chatted at the river, loud enough so that you could hear them on the other side. Your dad knew exactly when your mum lost her soap in the river. That was back then, when Pinbauê was still a small village, and the water of the Velho Chico was still clean," Uncle Flores told me.

*fishermen   ** launderers

"But then, the factory was built and a lot of people came to the village," Uncle Flores continued. "Construction workers, truck drivers, tractor drivers, engineers, and men in dark suits. Houses had to be built for the people. Big houses and small houses. Pinbauê grew and grew, bit by bit. That's how our village became a town."
For as long as I can remember, everyone in Pinbauê worked in the factory, except for Uncle Flores and my dad. He said: "I'm a fisherman, and I will always be a fisherman, until the river doesn't give me a single fish anymore." But my mum said that we would only have one small fish to eat every day if she didn't work in the factory.

"When I grow up, I want to be a tailor. That is a good job," I said to
my uncle one day.
"You are right, Edinho. But I wish I could sew colorful clothes again.
For a long time now I have only been sewing gray work clothes for
the factory."
That was true, Uncle Flores sewed gray overalls day in, day out.
And I also had been cutting and ironing only gray fabric for
a long time.

A short time later I noticed that my uncle hadn't sewn any gray
work clothes for a while.
"Uncle Flores hasn't had anything to do lately," I told my mum
at home.
She told me what had happened in the factory: "A couple of weeks ago,
a deliveryman brought parcels from abroad. They contained work
clothes, and now we all wear these new overalls. Some have come apart
already. But they don't get repaired, you just get new ones."

Soon after, Uncle Flores got a call from the factory. They didn't
need him anymore, because they could now buy cheaper work
clothes abroad.
"How can it be that someone can sew cheaper than me?
Who are these tailors?" Uncle Flores asked and shook his head.

Even if it hadn't been fun always sewing gray uniforms, now Uncle
Flores was worried because he didn't have any work. On the other
hand, he had time to go for walks with me.
From the shore of the river we watched Dad throwing his net into
the water and reeling it back in. Uncle Flores looked over the
river: "The factory has changed our village completely. Every house
in Pinbauê is covered with gray dust these days. There have only
been small fish in your dad's net for a long time, and the women can't
wash their clothes in the murky river anymore."
It was on one of these walks that I mentioned to my uncle that I had
found something interesting in the chest of drawers in his house. But
my uncle was lost in thought and did not seem to hear.

Only when we got back home did Uncle Flores ask me what
it was I had found in the drawers.
"There are lots of colorful materials. You told me that you used
to sew beautiful dresses for ladies and fancy suits for men.
Even carnival people ordered your costumes, didn't they?
You could turn these materials into colorful curtains."
Uncle Flores looked at me for a while and then he told me:
"That's not a bad idea, Edinho."
On that very day he was back at his sewing machine.
Cloc cloc cloc cloc cloc cloc cloc.

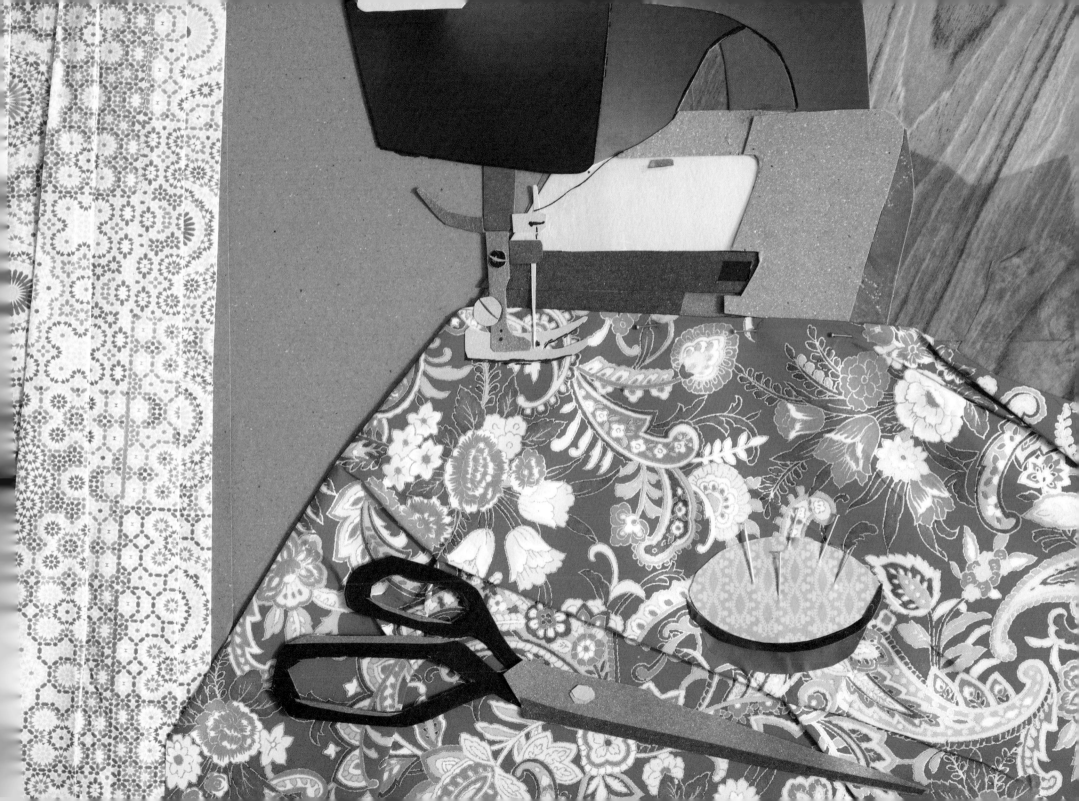

The next weekend we went to the Praça Central* to sell our curtains.
Uncle Flores took his small horse and was escorted by
one of the many viralatas.**
I went by foot with my wheelbarrow, which was loaded to the top.
I arrived soaked in sweat, but there was no time for a rest.

Uncle Flores stuck his broom between two
trees and hung up the curtains.
It didn't take too long before Doña
Beija stopped by. She bought
a curtain for her popcorn stand.
Her customers admired the
colorful curtains—and that was
how it all started.

*central square   ** stray dog

All around Praça Central, and soon all over Pinbauê, you could see colorful curtains in the windows. It became obvious to everyone: something was changing in Pinbauê. People now looked out their windows again; some even painted their homes in a bright color. And there was even more change: people started to order shirts and dresses from Uncle Flores again. They ordered colorful clothes for parties, weddings, and birthdays. . .

And that's how Uncle Flores's house became the most popular in
Pinbauê. On some days you would find a long line in front of
the building.
The customers liked to stay for a *cafezinho* with *broa** and more
often than not they ended up in a long conversation with my uncle.
One day, after the last customer had left the shop, I said to Uncle Flores:
"The people in Pinbauê used to look so serious. Now, when they
leave with their new clothes they seem to be in such a good mood.
What is it you actually do?"
"I make clothes, offer a good cafezinho and a nice broa, and I listen
to what the people have to say."
"Is that all?" I asked.
"That's all indeed," said Uncle Flores.

*coffee and corn cake

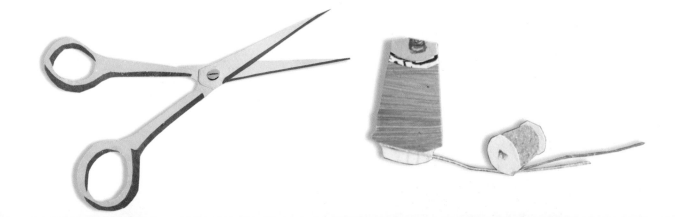

That was quite a few years ago. Now I sit at the sewing machine myself and make the suits, shirts, and dresses according to the wishes of the people in Pinbauê. Yes, I did become a tailor too.
Uncle Flores is very happy, though his eyesight is now failing. However, he still welcomes the customers and invites them for a cafezinho and a chat. . .

Afterword

Pinbauê may be an invented name, but this story has been inspired by many true incidents. Pinbauê could have been one of many small cities in the state of Minas Gerais in Brazil. Like many cities in my home state, Pinbauê is covered with dust from the chimneys of factories. The soil in Minas Gerais is very rich in iron and others minerals. That has lured lots of factories to the region in the last decade. They offer a lot of work, but they do a lot of damage to nature. Velho Chico is the nickname for the river São Francisco. It is the longest river in Brazil and its spring is in Minas Gerais. This river has been suffering for years now because of the pollution from industry, and now people are even planning on re-routing the river to the dry northeast of Brazil. Many fear an ecological catastrophe.

Edinho's father and uncle have jobs that are slowly vanishing from daily life. They love nature and the Velho Chico and try to keep up the traditional lifestyle. Edinho's mother thinks practically, like many women in Brazil. They work hard and their workdays are long. Because of this many children grow up with relatives or friends. Not all of them are lucky enough to have an uncle like Mr. Flores near them.

Edinho is the one who has the idea that is really important to his uncle. And that too is typical of life in Brazil: people have to learn to find answers to problems at a young age. They live in a country that is constantly changing and where everything is provisional. You need good ideas to survive.

There is a saying in Brazil that expresses the Brazilian way of life: "The future is now." You don't think much about tomorrow. Maybe that explains the Brazilian lifestyle known around the world. And maybe that's why Brazil is known as the country of festivals and parties: birthdays, weddings, baptisms, Carnival, festivals for every saint, and even an All Saints' Day. Nobody knows what will happen tomorrow. That's why we should celebrate today.

And of course festive clothes are important for every one of these occasions. It doesn't matter if you are rich or poor, Brazilians always have something fancy to wear.

Uncle Flores is concerned about the factory on the other side of the river. He knows that the men in the dark suits have a lot of power. They are the ones that construct the big factories and make decisions that affect the future of the people in Pinbauê. Edinho and his uncle are determined to change something. The solution they find may not bring back the fresh air, the clean water, or the fish, but it gives the people hope and happiness. And that's quite a beginning, isn't it?

Eymard Toledo, February 2017